Mr Creep the crook was a bad man.
Mrs Creep the crook was a bad woman.
Miss Creep and Master Creep
were bad children,
and "Growler" Creep was a bad dog.

For some of the time Mr Creep
and his family lived in a secret den.
For the rest of the time
they lived in jail.

Mr Creep the Crook

the

Crook

Ahlberg & Amstutz

PUFFIN BOOKS
UK | USA | Canada | Ireland | Australia
India | New Zealand | South Africa
Puffin Books is part of the Penguin Random House group of companies
whose addresses can be found at global.penguinrandomhouse.com.

puffinbooks.com

First published in hardback by Viking and in paperback by Puffin Books 1988
This edition published 2015
001
Text copyright © Allan Ahlberg, 1988
Illustrations copyright © André Amstutz, 1988
Educational Advisory Editor: Brian Thompson
The moral right of the author and illustrator has been asserted
A CIP catalogue record for this book is available from the British Library
Made and printed in China
ISBN: 978–0–723–29770–3

One day Mr Creep was sitting
in his little jail-house.
He was drinking a cup of jail-house tea
and eating a piece of jail-house cake
and planning how to get out.

Here is Mr Creep's plan.

Mrs Creep was knitting a jail-house jumper.
When she saw the plan, she said,
"That's a nice plan – can we stop
at a wool shop?"
"And a sweet shop, too!" the children said.
But Mr Creep shook his head.
"No," he said. "No changes to the plan –
it's fool-proof!"

A few weeks later, this happened.
As you can see, the plan
was fool-proof — well, nearly.

The next day
Mr Creep was sitting on the sand.
He was eating a seaside sandwich,
and drinking a bottle of seaside beer
and planning how to get-rich-quick.

Bike

Seaside

Here is Mr Creep's plan.

Mrs Creep was being buried
in the sand by the children.
When she saw the plan, she said,
"That's a *very* nice plan –
but you forgot the wool shop!"

Then, a few days later, this happened.

The Creeps got biffed
by Mr Biff,

and had their bottoms burned
by Mrs Plug.

Mr Cosmo the conjuror
played a trick on them.

Mrs Wobble the waitress dropped a jelly on them.

They got stung by bees,

kicked by a horse and chased by cops.

By mistake, they also burgled
a burglar – and *he* robbed *them*!
And besides all that – it snowed.

"Was that a fool-proof plan, too, dad?"
the children said.
And Mr Creep said, "No."

A few hours later
Mr Creep was sitting in his secret den.
He was drinking a glass of secret water,
and sticking a secret plaster on his nose.
Also, he was dreaming
of his cosy jail-house ...
and planning how to get back *in*!
Here is Mr Creep's plan.

Seaside

Stolen car

Getting 'Back in' plan

"This time it really is
a fool-proof plan," he said.
And it was.

Now, as you have seen,
Mr Creep the crook was a bad man.
Mrs Creep the crook was a bad woman.
Miss Creep and Master Creep
were bad children,
and "Growler" Creep was a bad dog.

However, most things change,
as time goes by.
So, after a year or two,
the Creeps were not quite so bad.
And after another year,
they were nearly good.
And after six more months,
they *were* good.

At last they were let out of jail.

The next day
Mr Creep was sitting up in bed.
He was drinking a cup of home-made coffee
and eating a slice of home-made toast
and planning his last plan.

Being good — final plan

Mr Creep

get a job

Lollipop Man

Mrs Creep

get a job

WOOL Dept

Sales lady

Master & Miss Creep

go to School

Top of class

Growler

well trained

When Mrs Creep and the children
saw the plan, they said,
"That's the best plan of all!"
"It's perfect, dad!"
"It's fool-proof!"
And so it was...

. . . well, nearly.

The End

For my sister, Pauline

T. M.

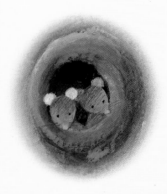

ORCHARD BOOKS
96 Leonard Street, London EC2A 4XD
Orchard Books Australia
32/45-51 Huntley Street, Alexandria, NSW 2015
ISBN 1 84121 468 X (hardback)
ISBN 1 84362 287 4 (paperback)
First published in Great Britain in 2003
First paperback publication in 2004
Text and illustrations © Tony Maddox 2003
The right of Tony Maddox to be identified as
the author and illustrator of this work
has been asserted by him in accordance with
the Copyright, Designs and Patents Act, 1988.
A CIP catalogue record for this book is
available from the British Library.
(hardback) 10 9 8 7 6 5 4 3 2 1
(paperback) 10 9 8 7 6 5 4 3 2 1
Printed in Dubai

Not so loud, Oliver!

Tony Maddox

ORCHARD BOOKS

It was night-time
on Mulberry Farm.
Time to sleep for all
the baby animals.

Everywhere was
still and quiet.

The cows were snoring softly in the barn.

The chicks were cuddled up cosily in the henhouse

and the ducklings were dreaming gently amongst the reeds.

Too-Wit
Too-Woo!

But high up in the
roof of the oldest barn,
Oliver Owl wasn't sleepy.
He stretched his wings and
gave a loud, "Too-wit, Too-woo!"

"MOO!" called Mamma Cow from below.

"Shhh, not so loud Oliver! My little calves are sleeping."

Oliver practised being quieter.
In the softest of soft
voices he sang,

"Cluck! Cluck!" called Mamma Hen from the henhouse.

"Shhh, not so loud Oliver! It's my little chicks' bedtime."

So Oliver tried one last time. In the smallest of small voices he whispered,

"Quack, quack!"
called Mamma Duck
from the duckpond.

"Shhh, not so loud Oliver!
My little ducklings are sleepy."

Oliver gave a sigh,
and flew up, up, up to
the branches of his favourite
oak tree. There he sat silently
while the farmyard animals
slept down below.

But what was that dark shape creep, creep, creeping towards the henhouse?

It was Foxy Fox, and he was looking for his evening meal!

Closer and closer he crept,

past the duckpond, around the barn

and right up to the henhouse door.

Oliver had to do something
– and quick! He flapped
his wings as fast
as he could . . .

It was so loud that it
woke Mamma Cow
who started to "MOO!"

It was so loud that it woke Mamma Hen who started to

"Cluck!"

And it was so loud that it woke Mamma Duck who started to

"Quack!"

Oliver's voice was
so loud that it scared
Foxy Fox right away.

And from then on, nobody
minded Oliver's singing . . .

Too-Wit Too-Woo!

Well, not much!